A Nice Place To Visit

Charles Goldberg, M.D.

iUniverse, Inc.
New York Bloomington

A Nice Place To Visit

iUniverse books may be ordered through booksellers or by contacting:

iUniverse
1663 Liberty Drive
Bloomington, IN 47403
www.iuniverse.com
1-800-Authors (1-800-288-4677)

ISBN: 978-1-4502-7588-0 (sc)
ISBN: 978-1-4502-7589-7 (ebk)

Printed in the United States of America

iUniverse rev. date: 05/23/2011

This book is lovingly dedicated to my fiancé, Rina.

I would like to gratefully acknowledge the contributions of my sons, Benjamin and Jesse, and the tireless work of my secretary, Tami White.

Contents

The Poetry Reading

The Salon was founded in 1976 as the first multipurpose literary center focused on providing support for writers at all stages of their development in the Washington DC suburbs. Workshops were based on the apprenticeship model. At first, the Salon was located in an abandoned school. Then in an old amusement park next to a merry-go-round and pottery and craft shops. Then in an office on top of a lighting store. And finally in a building that had been used by Montgomery County's Rec Department. Aside from drunks coming in for a drink and occasional upper middle-class housewives coming in for a "cut and blow-dry," visitors to the Salon were expected to write. Poets, novelists, biographers, and short-story writers came in from their real lives as housewives, computer programmers, rehab techs, teachers, and waiters.

Chuck Goldbug usually could not go to his wife's poetry readings. They were mostly on Sunday afternoons and conflicted with Eagles games. This particular Sunday the Eagles were not playing, a fact that Goldbug had concealed.

They arrived early so Beverly could plan the reading with her sister poets. Goldbug hovered around the entrance, watching the people come in. The women wore colorful outfits, a lot of purple and silver and orange, and stones—shiny stones, odd-shaped stones, big purple stones, little yellow stones, big turquoise stone—on necklaces and bracelets and sometimes just hanging by themselves. They also were adorned with scarves and capes and pashminas and boots, high and shiny and dark.

1

So the typical poetess showed up wearing a long, dark skirt, black boots, a lot of the requisite stones and a light blouse, incompletely wrapped in a purple cape. The uniform resembled that of a social worker.

The reading was called to order by a man wearing glasses and a short beard who was dressed like a truck driver. He wore old, dirty work shoes, dungarees, and a Mets jersey. He had the look of a man searching for the kind of easy masculinity that had always eluded him. His name was Sheldon Paskevitz. He and his wife, Audry—who looked just like him— had founded the Salon twenty-five years ago. They were refugees from New York and wanted to incorporate many of the ideas behind the 92nd Street "Y". Both of them were frustrated writers. Sheldon was around more beautiful women after organizing the Salon than ever before, which, of course, ultimately led to their divorce. The final irony was that after a lifetime of their upholding literary standards, the best seller that their son wrote was a biography of the Monkees.

There is a tradition in poetry readings at the Salon—usually three poets read from their works. The first reader was a tall, zaftig woman with wide-spaced eyes, long, dark hair, and a tendency not to look at people in the eye. When she was introduced, she was applauded and one could hear all the stones clicking. She was the divorced wife of a psychoanalyst. When she would say something in a particularly artful way, the audience would respond with a collective "ooh" and then "ahh." While she was speaking, the audience was silent, paying rapt attention, which made the oohs and ahhs more emphatic.

Goldbug was seated at the end of a middle row. He could not stop fidgeting. His chair would creak, and thirty pairs of eyes stared at him with disapproving glances. So he slinked back to the rear.

Standing in the back, he would meet Beverly's friends as they came in. He saw Kimmy Aragon looking none the worse after her recent divorce. That marriage had been a real happening, a Shinto ceremony to her Japanese lover who had bought the condo unit adjacent to her own, knocked down the wall, and laid out a beautiful, huge living space with windows, great views of Washington DC, shrines, and much empty space—particularly valuable to a Japanese person used to being crowded and cramped. But after six weeks, Kimmy stalked out and Chuck joked to Beverly that Takeo was going to commit hara-kiri.

Apparently, Kimmy had refused to sleep with Takeo for six weeks after the wedding, saying he was treating her differently after the wedding, as if she *had* to sleep with him. Takeo said, "Isn't that what marriage is supposed to be?", which is when she left. All of Kimmy's poet friends empathized with her about Takeo's insensitivity. Chuck wanted to know if Takeo was going to sublet space, to which Beverly replied that if he didn't shut up, pretty soon he would need to sublet some space. Takeo was last seen on an ANA flight to Tokyo, mumbling incoherently about American women.

Chuck also saw Jocelyn Plantar, the one poet friend Beverly had whom Chuck really liked. She was cute, unpretentious, and had the kind of sexy, raspy voice that reminded him of Tallulah Bankhead or Judy Davis. Her husband, Weldon Plantar III, nicknamed Soapy, was a hardworking, blue-collar guy who fixed and installed cable systems. No one knew he came from a wealthy family, that his father had lost the business by gambling all his money away, and that Soapy went from being an athletic, privileged sports car-racing prep school rascal to working sixty hours a week to support his mother. After she died, he met Jocelyn and the two of them were very happy.

When the tall woman had received her final oohs and ahhs, it was Beverly's turn. No far-off glance for her. She scrambled up the stage steps and reveled in the limelight. She always said her ambition in life was to be on "The Dick Cavett Show." Perhaps her chronic depression, manifested by her less colorful uniform, came from Cavett's show being canceled without her ever making it on.

"Take care where your foot falls, for that's where your mouth fills." "Ooh." "Ahh."

Afterward, Beverly asked Chuck how he enjoyed it. He said he enjoyed it in the sense that it was a happening but he could not appreciate the emphasis on words.

"Too many obsessive women. They look like they should be hysterical with all their colorful outfits and jewelry, and then they spend all their time listening and thinking. What a waste."

"You want them to dance for you?"

"Yes, and if you want a literary reference, try Laban's daughters dancing for Jacob in the red tent."

Charles Goldberg, M.D.

Sometimes Beverly did not mind such remarks and might even be amused by his flagrant primitivism, but this time she got very annoyed, probably because he had been insufficiently complimentary about her reading.

Her reaction left Chuck with an ominous feeling in the pit of his stomach.

The Office

The room was shaped like a railroad car—long and thin, with a row of five black, padded metal chairs along the long wall opposite the entry door. At either end were soft, brown, fuzzy-barrel easy chairs. Above one was a wooden coat rack. Above the other was an Israeli tile print of two figures dancing. There was track lighting in the ceiling along with two speakers. Between the fifth chair and the door to the office was a brown, plastic table holding a brown table lamp. Behind the lamp was a colorful Dale Terbush print of an underwater tableau with fish and flora, picked up in the Hillcrest section of San Diego to match the centerpiece of the waiting room—a six-foot, one hundred and fifty-pound stuffed golden dusky shark caught two hundred yards off North Miami Beach in a forty-minute struggle capped by a rifle shot by the frenetic Brooklyn-born captain who explained, "You think I'm crazy enough to let a live shark on my boat?" The stuffed shark was especially upsetting to two categories of Dr. Goldbug's patients—animal-loving vegetarians and lawyers.

At right angle to the Israeli print was a brown, orange, and silver geometric abstract picked up from a furniture store in downtown Washington—an abstract uniquely made from paper towels. By the foot of one barrel chair was a magazine holder stuffed with an eclectic mix of *Newsweek* (with the area of the front page containing the home address label torn off), three copies of *Esquire*, *Reader's Digest*, and *Parenting*, and the occasional but inevitable *People*.

The patient was a tall and dark woman, sitting poised and almost frozen in the chair right by the magazines, at the boundary between young womanhood and young matronhood.

The door opened and in a friendly and warm tone, which belied the thousands of times it had been said, a stocky, bearded man with casual tan slacks, a blue shirt, and a striped blue and tan tie said, "Won't you come in?"

Mrs. Harriet Harrison was the older of two girls, born to a lawyer and his homemaker wife. She was five years older than her sister. The father was very prominent and an attractive, dynamic man. He and his wife went out a lot, and Mrs. Harrison had to babysit for her younger sister. This lasted even until the teenage years. She never was serious with anyone until the last year of community college, having stayed at home caring for her sister most of the time. When she met her husband, a graduate student, she dropped out of school. They got married, and soon after that she was pregnant.

When Mrs. Harrison presented herself originally for treatment in a mental health center, she was a forty-year-old mother of two teenage daughters and married for nineteen years. Her husband was a successful business executive recently promoted to a very high position, whose frequent traveling left his wife alone. She became very anxious whenever she tried to leave the house. Her daughters were out a lot and her husband was almost never home. Her anxiety was manifested by sweating, a quickened heartbeat, fearfulness, and butterflies in her stomach.

When she was alone, she'd clean the house, polish the furniture, vacuum all the rooms, even counted the birds that flew by. She felt trapped, just like a prisoner. She had been placed in a women's group to raise her consciousness about how women were oppressed and to try to liberate her from her domestic chains.

She got worse. The anxiety attacks became more severe and more frequent. Desperate, she left the women's group and came to see Dr. Goldbug, who felt that the women's group had dealt with superficial external factors but not with what was going on inside the patient's psyche. That approach reminded Dr. Goldbug of a patient who had come to see a psychiatrist and said he had to get away. The psychiatrist called the airlines. The women's group had encouraged Mrs. Harrison to think that the problem was outside herself, so there was really no work for her to do. She got a lot of sympathy. There was a lot of scapegoating. Her problems were blamed on others. She did not have to take responsibility for her own conflicts.

Goldbug felt that the answer was inside, that her mother's second pregnancy came in the middle of Mrs. Williamson's oedipal infatuation with her father. In addition to normal sibling rivalry, her sister's arrival symbolized her defeat, her "losing" her father to her mother. Although she loved her little sister, nurtured her, and took pride in her assertiveness, her confidence, and her precocious social skills, the patient must have also resented her. Like most people, she had trouble with normal ambivalence and felt guilt about resenting someone she loved, which is the psychodynamic core of depression. She had to cover up her resentment by taking really good care of her, being very nice to her, and almost dedicating her life to her—just like she later did with her own girls.

Mrs. Harrison used to give up dates to stay home to take care of her sister. Her sister dated more in high school than she did in college. The same pattern was repeated with her daughters: to go out, even without her husband, and leave her daughters was equivalent in her mind to killing them, which is how she felt—killed—when her mother went out with her father and she was left at home.

Still, Dr. Goldbug had put her on two medications, one to prevent the anxiety attacks and another to mitigate them. In three months her anxiety attacks had decreased and she had begun leaving the house on short trips.

He asked Mrs. Harrison to come in. Dr. Goldbug held the door. As she entered, Mrs. Harrison bent down and picked up several pieces of mail the mailman had left on the carpet. She handed them to the psychiatrist, and then they both sat down.

Mrs. Harrison began. "Well, I drove my one daughter to ballet and the other to school. Last night they were both visiting friends. They are so busy. They don't seem to have time to clean their room. They just leave their things lying on the floor."

"Like my floor?"

Staring at the mail he set on the desk, Mrs. Harrison responded, "Well, ah, you mean your mail. That's not your fault—that's where the mailman left it."

"Sounds like you're defending me."

"What? Dr. Goldbug, sometimes I have a hard time understanding you. How am I defending you? I am just sure that you are quite busy, just like my husband. He ran out of the house so fast this morning, he left this important envelope on the table. I barely caught him as he was driving off. I guess I'm like a mailman—giving letters to you and my husband!"

"Delivering your children?" he offered.

Mrs. Harrison was smiling as she shot back, "That's more like special delivery!"

"A mailman carries a heavy load."

Mrs. Harrison stopped smiling and started to fidget in her chair. "Well, everybody works hard," she said as she fumbled in her pocketbook and took out a cigarette. While nervously puffing on it, she rambled on. "I remember when I was little, we had this mailman, Mr. Docherty. He was so nice. He used to give all the dogs on our street cookies. You know, so they wouldn't bite him, and he used to give out candy cigarettes to the kids."

"You just lit a cigarette," Dr. Goldbug pointed out.

Mrs. Harrison was silent for a moment. Then she started to cry. "I used to wait for him. My father would go away on these business trips. Sometimes he would send me postcards. When there wouldn't be any, I would have one of Mr. Docherty's candy cigarettes. I wouldn't eat it all at once. I would eat some of it and then like ... save it. It would last for hours."

She was silent for a moment and then inquired, "Dr. Goldbug, aren't you going to say anything or ask me something?"

"Sometimes you feel I am not with you?" he asked

"I guess I really miss my father, like I miss my husband, and I want you to say more too. I don't know what about ... but something." She was crying again. "Everybody is always leaving. They leave me holding the bag like a mailman." Fighting back the tears, she smiled and concluded, "That's something that you would say."

The Home

Chuck parked his car in the street beside the front-to-back split level, which was sitting on a hill, next to the woods, across from the school. He walked into the door. Bart and Jason were lying on the floor in front of the TV. He heard Beverly banging pots and pans in the kitchen.

"Daddy!" they cried and rushed toward him. A mélange of hugs and yelps and happy cries followed as they both jumped on him, and the three of them collapsed onto the blue tiles of the foyer.

"Wait, wait. I have to get into my play clothes," Chuck said, awkwardly getting up and walking into the kitchen to kiss his wife hello and ask, "What's for dinner?"

"Oh, is that your first thought?" she said with a smile on her lips.

Chuck joked, "Yes, Harriet. Ozzie's home after having worked hard all day."

"Capon," she announced, "and we have to eat soon. There's a meeting at the Salon tonight."

As he changed into his old clothes, Chuck remembered their first meeting during his psych residency at Sheppard-Pratt. Marty, his fellow Psychiatric Resident, and his wife had invited him to dinner to meet an old friend of theirs from New York who was coming for a weekend of solace in Baltimore to get away from a painful divorce. Chuck had put a Japanese bathrobe over his jeans and jumped into his convertible. "I Beg Your Pardon (I Never Promised You a Rose Garden)" was on the radio. He came into their house and did his sumo wrestler routine, stomping around the floor. Claudia threw some rice on him and said, "How'd you know we were having rice?" Marty leaned over him and made some cryptic comment, like, "Oh, you want Beverly to know right away you're somewhat eccentric."

Beverly had been surprisingly attractive—short, dark, curvy, smiling more and more as the evening went on, allowing her taut, symmetrical, melancholic features to relax. After Marty and Claudia had gone to bed, they made love in their friends' living room, with Chuck exclaiming, "Beverly!" at the moment of climax. Beverly told him later that she had known they would when, after he tried to kiss her on an after-dinner walk, he had said to her, "I guess you don't know me very well." She said later that it was the only time in their whole relationship he had spoken her name during sex.

"Daddy, what's taking so long?" His reverie interrupted, Chuck jumped down the few stairs and said, "Let's go outside." As he raked the leaves in the backyard near the swing set, which was the apogee of his usually limited handyman life, the kids jumped gleefully into knee-high piles of leaves he kept trying to form.

Chuck felt a warm glow remembering the doctor who had told him, "I'm sorry, you'll never have children. Normal sperm count is seventy to one hundred million, and you only have eight." The surgery he had for his varicocele during his internship had only increased it to fifteen million. So he was surprised that evening at the Polynesian restaurant when Beverly had slipped him a Father's Day card.

Bart had been conceived during a bout of makeup loving at the Fort Campbell, Kentucky Guest House, where they had gone after their fantastic English honeymoon to find a place to live for the next two years. They had been fighting about whether Beverly was going to work. Jason had been conceived two years later in the den on their sleep-sofa with Beverly's dog, Mona, sniffing in close proximity. Chuck laughed out loud. Even if they weren't adorable, precocious, athletic, loving kids, he would still think they were the best thing he had ever done.

Later that night after two sock fights, four books, drop four, a soccer game, and popcorn, the kids finally went to bed. Beverly came home obsessing about two poetry lines—"Watch where you step, you'll fall where you slip." After two hours with much input from Chuck and each word having to endure ruthless scrutiny, the two lines became, "Take heed where your foot falls, for that's where your mouth fills." Grateful for his jaw-clenching patience, Beverly initiated lovemaking. Chuck then fell into a deep sleep, which was shattered about 4 AM by a phone call from the hospital. He groped for the phone with clumsy gross motor movements as sleep slowly yielded.

A female voice almost triumphantly said, "Dr. Goldbug, you're on call tonight. The doctor wants to talk to you."

The nurse transferred the phone to the doctor, who continued, "Dr. Goldbug, this is Jack Smythe in the ER. We have a young man in here that's violently agitated. He's threatening staff with a chair at this point. We'd like you to come in and see him."

"Okay, be there in a little while."

Dr. Smythe offered, "Thanks … I'm sorry," before he hung up.

The Emergency Room

Goldbug arrived at the hospital in forty minutes. There were no parking spaces. There was a freshly mowed lawn, several bushes, and a no-parking sign. Two blocks away he found a parking lot with no vacancies. Four blocks away he found another parking lot and was about to enter it, but he suddenly turned his car around, drove near the emergency room entrance, and parked on the grass.

As he walked in, a nurse said, "You must be Dr. Goldbug. Don't you believe in staying off the grass?"

Exasperated, Goldbug responded, "What is this—a greenhouse or a hospital? People need a place to park."

"Don't you believe in living, growing things?" the nurse asked.

Goldbug shot back, "Do you water these plants or take their vital signs? Are you here to take care of people or plants?"

The nurse, notably discomfited, explained the situation. "Well, this young man Dr. Smythe called you about, he came in with his mother. Now he is violently threatening everybody. He's in the cubicle over there with his chair. We tried to talk him down but he just got more agitated. Dr. Smythe had gone over him physically when he first came in and couldn't find anything. We have a urine for drugs pending."

She led him through the emergency room and came to a small area half enclosed with curtains where a tall, heavyset black man was standing on top of a bed, brandishing a chair, cursing, drooling, and gesturing in an angry way.

Goldbug turned to the nurse and asked if she knew what Code Green was. She said, "Yes, that is when all the male aides from psych and all the security guards are called in."

Goldbug told her to call one. The nurse asked, "Don't you even want to talk to him?"

"Nope. If I thought what he needed was persuasion, I'd have you call a law student. What he needs is control. Draw up a syringe of 100 mg Thorazine."

Just then an elderly black woman approached Goldbug. "You the doctor? I'm Mrs. Jefferson. This is my son James. I have been trying to get help for him for a week. He's been acting funny—getting up at night, wandering around, yelling and cursing, talking to himself, even screaming at me. He stopped going to work. I called the police but they said they could not do anything. I called my doctor. He gave me some pills. They didn't help. The only way I got him to come here was to say that if he didn't come he couldn't stay with me anymore. He started cursing at me but he got in the cab when I told him to. He was quiet at first, but as soon as the nurses started asking him questions, he blew up and said he was going to kill someone … that people were sucking him dry in some experiment and he was gonna fight back. Then he threw one of his boots at me. Doc, can't you help him? He needs help real bad."

Goldbug attempted to reassure her. "Mrs. Jefferson, we'll try. He needs to be calmed down and hospitalized. It will be against his will, so he'll have to be committed. Then he'll get the help he needs."

With a sigh of relief, Mrs. Jefferson exclaimed, "Lordy, I'm glad someone is going to help him. Doc, he even talked about killing me, his own mother."

"Has he ever talked like that before?" he asked.

"Not like that," she said. "Always been quiet. Never messed much with people. Never hung around with girls. No gangs. No drugs. He watched a lot of TV, and when working at the warehouse he kept mostly to himself."

"Any allergies?"

"No."

"Any history of mental illness in the family? And, by the way, how old is he?"

"Eighteen. His daddy was in the hospital once down south. He stayed for about a half a year. Then, when James was three, his daddy was killed in a fight in a bar. His daddy was always fighting. After that, we came up north, but he has never been like this before … always been real good and done what I said. You know, Doc, when they're little, they step on your feet. When they're big, they step on your heart."

The nurse approached Goldbug and Mrs. Jefferson, followed by eight husky men, some dressed in white and some in blue. Goldbug asked the nurse to lead Mrs. Jefferson away. He addressed the men.

"What we are about to do is to subdue this troubled young man without his getting hurt and without our getting hurt. I will approach him with a mattress. You four over there mobilize his legs and the lower part of his body, and you four do the same with his arms. At the count of three, we will rush him. Any questions? Okay."

Goldbug picked up a mattress from a nearby bed and approached James, who noticed this and screamed, "What do you want, you motherfucker?"

"One, two, three," Goldbug counted before he rushed James with the mattress over his head. The patient bent down and hit the mattress with a chair. The other men rushed in and quickly immobilized James as he continued to scream and curse.

Goldbug shouted to the nurse, "Get that Thorazine over here!" The nurse approached the patient and quickly injected the drug.

James, lying on the bed and restrained by aides, screeched, "No, no. What you doing to me? Don't give me no needle! Help! They are poisoning me!"

Then, almost immediately, he started to cry as he quieted down. Within ten minutes he was asleep.

The nurse asked Goldbug, "Do you want the commitment papers?"

"Yes, and make out a separate sheet for the ER doc. He told me he'd be glad to sign."

The nurse went on. "And doctor, there are three people who want to see you. There's a Mr. Harry Apple—"

"Who's he?" Goldbug asked.

"He is with a group that opposes involuntary commitment," she said.

Goldbug teased, "Well, maybe we can arrange for Mr. Jefferson to spend the night at Mr. Apple's house."

Smiling, the nurse patted Goldbug on the arm and continued.

"There's also a Mrs. Gannon from the psych unit and a Mr. Stanley Plotkin from the Medicaid HMO."

"Do you have a room?" he asked.

"Yes." she said. "Follow me. I'll get the commitment papers. Who should I send in?"

"Let's start with Mr. Apple."

A well-dressed, tall, thin, bearded man came into the room. "Apple. Dr. Goldbug, I presume."

"That's right," he said

"I am Harry Apple of the Mental Health and Liberties Project. I see you are about to send someone else to one of your psychiatric prisons."

While writing, Goldbug replied, "If you mean we are trying to prevent someone from killing his mother and trying to get him to accept treatment that will end some of his suffering, then … yes."

Apple declared, "How long will you be abusing your power? How long are you planning to keep him?"

"That depends on how he does."

"Did this guy try to hurt his mother? Did he attack her?"

"No. He just verbally threatened her."

Apple went on. "Don't psychiatrists recognize freedom of speech?"

Goldbug tried to explain. "Look, his mother is not even concerned about herself, although she should be. She just wants to get her son some help."

Apple was clearly incensed. "Well, he sure got help—a gang assault, a shot in the butt, unlawful restraint."

"He's not sane," Goldbug replied. "He's not in reality. He's suffering from a major mental illness."

Apple smirked. "Well, it's not always convenient for the family. Give him an appointment to see a psychiatrist. Give him a chance to be treated."

Obviously tired, Goldbug tried again. "You don't understand. He doesn't think there's a reason to see anyone. He thinks people are out to hurt him. He's scared, so he strikes out."

"Well, none of your psychiatric labeling. If he hasn't done anything criminal, you have no right to hold him against his will."

"You don't recognize mental illness?" Goldbug asked.

Apple persisted. "I'm not impressed by psychiatric predictions or psychiatric mumbo jumbo. I'm going to have him out as soon as we can get a hearing."

Goldbug was trying to be patient. "You want him to have the right to kill someone or himself? That's what I'm trying to prevent."

"At the cost of his freedom?"

Incensed, Goldbug responded, "Well, which is more valuable? Freedom or life?"

"Until someone does something illegal, you have no right to take his freedom away."

Goldbug was now losing his patience. "Wait a minute. Medicine is not perfect. Twenty-five percent of all appendices taken out by surgeons are normal. If surgeons didn't operate on suspicions, many more people would die. You can't wait until it ruptures, and you can't wait until this fellow hurts somebody."

As Apple was walking away, he muttered, "You just can't take people's freedom away. Wait until he does something."

Raising his voice, Goldbug called out, "By then it'll be too late."

The nurse then came in and reminded Goldbug, "Doctor, there's still—"

"I know," he said. "Send in Mr. Plotkin."

A short, mustached man with glasses came in.

"Hi. I'm Dr. Chuck Goldbug."

"I'm Stanley Plotkin from the Medicaid HMO. I understand you plan to admit Mr. Jefferson."

Goldbug explained, "He is a paranoid schizophrenic who is going to kill his mother. He needs to be admitted for reasons of safety."

"Well, has he actually hurt his mother?" Plotkin asked.

"No, he threatened to, and he threatened hospital staff, and he is actually hallucinating with paranoid delusions."

"Well, Doctor, according to our admission criteria, you can only be admitted if you failed outpatient treatment, and he has never had any."

"Mr. Plotkin," Goldbug insisted, "this young man would never go to outpatient treatment."

"Doctor, do you know that for sure? You can't hospitalize everyone who makes a threat. We all say things."

"Did you see him? He is actively psychotic."

"Well, he needs medication."

"But he won't take medication," insisted Goldbug.

At this point, Plotkin backed off and advised, "Well, Doctor, you have to do what you think is right, but this will be referred to our Admissions Committee. You know, if you get a reputation as a trigger-happy psychiatrist who hospitalizes people willy-nilly, your membership in the HMO might come up for a review."

Goldbug just stared at him. Finally, he said, "Mr. Plotkin, you go ahead and do what you have to do."

As Plotkin left the office, Goldbug asked the nurse to bring in Mrs. Gannon.

A tall, grey-haired woman in a nurse's uniform entered. "Dr. Goldbug, I understand you want to admit Mr. Jefferson."

Goldbug answered, "Mrs. Gannon, I don't have a choice. He's a psychotic young man who is pretty bad off."

"Is he dangerous?"

"Yes."

"Well, then, I don't think he should go to our unit. He's too violent," she suggested.

But Goldbug persisted. "Mrs. Gannon, he's a paranoid schizophrenic who is decompensating and needs medication and supervision. There's no reason he can't be treated on the hospital's acute psych unit. He'll calm down pretty quickly."

"We have a lot of good people in that unit. Many of them are elderly. Some are depressed. They really can't tolerate much disruption."

"Mrs. Gannon, this young man has as much right as anyone to be on that unit. I know you have a peaceful, quiet, well-run unit, but you also have a lot of staff, a seclusion room if you need it, and the unit is certified to take people with acute psychotic disorders. How can we deal with discrimination against the mentally ill when some mentally ill want to set themselves up as superior to other mentally ill? Don't worry. I won't let him disrupt your unit."

At last Mrs. Gannon agreed. "Okay, Doctor, but you know he's different."

"Mrs. Gannon, he's no different than you or I would be if we had paranoid schizophrenia," he offered. Goldbug then finished his paperwork as the nurse sighed and left.

Group Therapy

The next day. Dr. Goldbug is sitting in one of the chairs arranged in a circle in a large conference room on the same floor of the hospital that the locked Psychiatric unit was on. A tall, blonde woman in a nurse's uniform sits in another chair. The door opens and nine teenagers pile in.

Cathy, an unattractive, slender girl of moderate height with a very loud laugh, spoke first. "Terry, sit here next to me. That's a real pretty outfit."

"Thank you," replied Terry, a striking blonde.

The sloppily dressed Stacey asked, "Where did you get it?"

"The boutique at the Plaza."

Susan, a well-built girl wearing jeans and a sweatshirt, cut in. "I go there sometimes."

Stacey continued, "So do I—mainly during school." All the girls laughed. "Really, it's not so crowded then."

"I know what you mean. The aisles are so narrow and when it's crowded, two people can't walk through at the same time," added Scott, a thick-cut, muscular boy with blonde hair.

Dr. Goldbug interjected, "So when you go to school and do what you're supposed to do, you feel crowded, like you don't have enough room to breathe."

Linda, a petite girl who looked ten or eleven, called out, "What? Put him in a hospital." Everyone laughed.

In a serious tone, Ronnie, an overweight boy in conventional clothes, explained, "It was the store that was crowded, not the school."

19

"Well, I know what he means," Susan countered. "At my school, there are these woods right outside, sort of a hangout. People go out and smoke pot between periods, sometimes during periods." Everyone laughed.

At this point Linda asked the group, "Anybody want to go down to the cafeteria for a soda?"

But Goldbug ignored the comment and continued. "Sometimes people feel crowded here."

"Somebody shut him up," Linda said.

"Please come," Terry asked the others.

"I'll go," Cathy said, and Stacey agreed, "So will I." All the girls but Susan got up and left.

Smiling, Scott brought up a new subject. "I almost got killed yesterday. Me and a friend were driving my parents' car. Well, really, I was driving. We were racing in the school parking lot. The other car was on our left. This wall was on our right, and all of a sudden ahead of us is this maintenance truck. I put on the brakes and stopped just inches from the truck. I mean inches!"

Speaking slowly and softly, Warren, an emaciated teen with hippie clothes and hair that covered his eyes, added, "Once I was riding my bike on this trail outside of my house. There was this creek, and we piled up dirt in front of the creek so you could sort of take off and jump over it. Anyway, I jumped the creek okay, but there was this log in the trail. I landed on the log, fell back into the creek, and broke my leg when my cycle landed on it."

"That reminds me of the second car I stole," said Greg, a tall, gangly boy.

Susan interrupted. "The second? What do you do, keep a file on them? Were there that many?"

Greg responded matter-of-factly. "Half a dozen. Well, I saw this cop, so I took the shortcut over this field but then took a bummer into the ditch. My head hit the dash and I broke my nose. I ran out of the car and went home. My dad wanted to know how I hurt my nose. I told him that I fell into a ditch, but I didn't mention anything about the car." The group started laughing.

Delving deeper, Goldbug inquired, "Do you wonder why people are hurting themselves?"

Scott took the lead. "I'm not trying to get hurt. It just happens. Last night I went up to the roof and closed my eyes and started walking. When I opened them, I was right on the edge. Just one more step and …"

Goldbug observed, "You really would have bitten the dust." Everyone laughed.

"Oh, no, not another pun," complained Susan.

Greg joked, "Like the old Western bad guys bit the dust."

Goldbug pressed on, "You think you are a bad guy, Scott, and that is why you are always punishing yourself, flirting with death."

"I'm not a bad guy. It's my dad who's the bad guy. He's always on my back … 'Do this, do that.' I come home from school the other day and the first thing he said was, 'Did you go to your classes?' I leave the house at night and he says, 'Don't do any drugs.' I come down to supper and he says, 'Is your room clean?' If he keeps it up, I'm going to punch him in the teeth."

Warren announced softly, "I've done that."

Gasping, Ronnie exclaimed, "What? To your father? Why?"

"Yeah, he was drunk again and yelling at my mother. I went in and told him to shut up. He swung at me and then I swung back. And then my mom pulled me away. I told him he'd better not bother my mom or any of us kids."

"My dad doesn't drink. He just hassles me," Scott said.

Greg then asked Warren, "How long has your father been drinking?"

"All of his life. He even—"

Just then the door opened. The four girls entered carrying sodas and junk food.

"Did we miss anything?" Stacey asked.

Linda joked, "I'll bet not."

There was a lot of laughter while various foods were passed around.

Susan then spoke, "Warren, you were saying something."

"Nah, I forgot," he said.

Stacey quickly changed the subject. "I broke up with my boyfriend last week."

"What happened?" Terry inquired.

"Well, I'd been going out with this guy for six months, and things were going pretty good. Then last month he went to Florida with his parents and stayed two weeks. That really pissed me off. Then this week is my class dance, and when he told me he would have to work that night, I called him a bastard. We had a fight and he asked me to give him back all of his comic books."

Terry acted surprised. "Comic books?"

"Yeah, he has this collection of Archie, Superman, Masked Marvel, and even Blackhawk. So I took some rocks, put them in a box, and sent them COD to him. He is expecting these comics, so he will accept the charges and then when he opens them up—"

Goldbug interjected, "You get your rocks off saying good-bye?"

"What do you mean?" Stacey asked.

"Well, you suffered disappointments, but were they grounds for general warfare?"

Smiling, Stacey explained, "Well, he left me. That's what he gets. I mean, my mother, after she married my stepfather, she retired from life. She will never leave him, the fat slob. All she does is drink. When she was with my real father, she would at least go out into the world and have a life. I will never get stuck like her."

"This my last corn chip, Dr. Goldbug. Do you want it?" Linda asked.

"No, thanks."

Linda was bothered. "You never take anything. We have some garden vegetables. I was going to offer you a cucumber, but I didn't know if Jews eat cucumbers."

Goldbug joked, "Only if they're covered with the blood of Christian children." The whole group laughed.

"I have a new boyfriend in school," said Susan.

Elbowing Stacey, Linda asked, "Does he give you comic books?"

Stacey asserted, "Well, I like comic books."

Susan continued, "No, but he's fourteen."

Terry yelled, "Fourteen? I'm fourteen and my boyfriend is seventeen, like you."

Susan retorted, "Well, he's not really my boyfriend. I just like to hang around with him. I don't know, there's something about younger guys that I like."

"I got caught shoplifting again," Terry began.

Stacey interrupted, "You bad, bad girl."

"Shoplifting?" Linda asked. "Why would you want to shoplift?"

Terry went on, "I don't know. I see something there and I just can't keep myself from taking it. This is the third time, and they tell me they're not going to dismiss the charges this time. They are gonna take it to court."

There ensued a general discussion of shoplifting and how not to get caught.

"Well, we have to stop now. See you all next week," Goldbug said.

The teenagers got up and left, saying their good-byes. Goldbug turned to the nurse he was supposed to train and started talking about the teenagers.

"It is a fairly verbal group we have right now. Sometimes everyone is kinda withdrawn or even schizoid, and it's hard to get anything going, but this is an extremely verbal group. Do you feel like talking about some of the people who particularly struck you?"

"I don't know," she replied. "They all seemed so healthy. They don't seem sick."

"Some people say that adolescence itself is a disease," Goldbug offered and continued to explain the group's history and progress.

"Warren talked about his father.

"Ronnie is the third of three boys born to an extremely dominating woman. She and her husband don't get along. She sort of involved herself with Ronnie, who's the baby of the family. Actually, she wasn't involved with the first two kids and they did pretty well. She really started overprotecting Ronnie, and as a result he became a mama's boy. He acts like a pseudo adult. He doesn't act like a teenager. You can tell by the clothes he wears. And actually, our main job was to try to get him to be more like a model teenager. He has been scapegoated in school. He is depressed and isolated. He is very bright. The other kids call him a bookworm. The teasing got so bad he had to transfer to a special school where no one knows how bright he is. He is very angry at his mother, but that is another story. And a lot of times a kid with his passivity is really sealing in a lot of rage.

"Susan has talked before in the group about the relationship between her mother and her father. Her mother is having an affair. Her father is sort of a passive guy who never leaves the house. He is overly involved with Susan. She has an older sister who got in trouble with drugs and is quite rebellious. Susan started out with some vague depression and hypochondria, but she has blossomed in the group somewhat. She is starting to get something out of it. She is becoming more aggressive and doesn't care so much what people think about her and is more willing to stand up for herself."

The nurse asked, "What is her thing about younger guys?"

Goldbug replied, "Well, it's almost impossible for her to relate to, you know, what you would call an appropriate young man. The anxiety from her relationship with her father and from what her mother has told her about men is so great that she deals with it by finding all these inappropriate characters. She even has crushes on men, like teachers in their thirties or forties, or else she goes out with these younger guys.

"Terry is unbelievable. As you can see, she does not look fourteen. She is fourteen going on thirty. The first night she came to the group her mother—and sometimes you wonder who is the mother and who is the daughter, her mother looks just like her—was making out with her newest boyfriend. We had to ask him to leave. The father was involved in drug smuggling and he was murdered. Her mother was sort of a flower child in the sixties. Terry and her sister never got much from her, just sort of lived from hand to mouth, traveling the drug circuit. She was raised in a commune at one point. Then, they went down to the Caribbean for some drug sales. They have moved all over. They don't have any money, and Terry has about as low a self-image as you can imagine. Even though she is very attractive and she is not dumb, she thinks the only way she's going to get anything from people is by stealing it."

Goldbug went on, "Stacey is a sharp kid. She is very mature for her age. Her mother is an alcoholic. She has a bad situation with her stepfather and a lot of stepbrothers and stepsisters. She is very rebellious, but there is so much hypocrisy in the home, it's hard to get her to respect herself. She doesn't respect anyone. She carries around a picture of her real father, who long ago left the scene. He was a sailor, and she has all sorts of fantasies about finding him. Of course, he was the first guy who left her, and she is kind of oversensitive to boyfriends leaving.

"Well, we're running out of time. We'll talk about the others next week."

Beverly

After Beverly dropped the kids off at Hebrew School, she had two hours until she had to pick them up. She had arranged with Claudia to meet her at the mall. But she was still laughing at something Bart and Jason had said—that the rabbi looked like Colonel Sanders of Kentucky Fried Chicken.

She had never seen herself as a mother. Chuck was so insistent on trying to have kids that she sometimes wondered if he had wanted her or he just wanted kids. What he had not known was what sad shape she was in when they married. He knew about the difficult divorce from Hans. Chuck called Hans the Dutch goy, as opposed to her sister, Mary's, first husband—the Filipino goy. That both girls first married ambitious, non-Jewish fortune hunters spoke to the secular nature of their home. Their father worshiped money. His wife worshiped manners—old European manners—in their refugee enclave in Queens. The Holocaust hung over their house like a cloud of toxic smoke; it never went away.

Beverly and Hans had lived in Europe and had an active social life. One of their friends was the pretender to the non-existent Portuguese throne. Hans had not wanted children. He said, "They interfere." They were hip, cynical, jaded, and as entitled as any of their friends.

Their social group was a model for a book published in France called "Chocolates for Breakfast." The book described a group of young, decadent European aristocrats who recognized no limits on what they wanted. If they wanted steak for breakfast instead of cereal and eggs, they had steak, and if they got tired of having to eat the steak to get to the dessert, they moved right to dessert and skipped the steak.

Chuck, with his nose for trivia, had read the book and used its lessons in his treatment of depressed, narcissistic adolescents.

He explained, "if a person could have whatever he wanted, if there were no limits, then whatever he had was never enough—because the person was always left with the possibility of wanting more. Limits were absolutely necessary for happiness; without limits a person could never be happy because he was always left thinking he could have or should have more than the next person. With no limits, nothing was ever enough. There was no avoiding the inevitable depression, which led to self-medication with drugs, which led to death. Truly, if everything was available, then nothing was acceptable … and, in fact, two of the members in Hans's and Beverly's social group had died of overdoses.

When Hans dumped her, it was like a kick in her stomach; but what Chuck did not know was that their relationship did not start that night he showed up in a Japanese bathrobe. He was funny and he made her laugh. She considered him a pleasant diversion, nothing more.

After that night she met Mark, whose wife had just committed suicide. Mark was the blackest person she had ever met. He saw everything through a lens of hopeless, bleak, nihilistic despair. His depression matched hers. They hit it off immediately and had a passionate six-month fling … until he shot himself, which was even more devastating than being dumped by Hans.

Beverly withdrew even more and needed more and more pot to get by.

Three months later, it was back to Marty and Claudia's in Baltimore. They asked her if she wanted to see Chuck and she said no, too complicated, so they enlisted a young, very nice Argentinean psychiatrist to take Beverly to the party they were going to.

The Argentinean was nice but boring. Chuck, who was at the party with a little Costa Rican redhead, who Beverly later liked to call the Whore of Babylon (which is what Beverly called any woman who looked at Chuck), reacted to her in a very restrained way. He said it was nice to see her and he hoped she was doing okay. No recriminations. No "Why didn't you call me?"

Compared to the drama of Hans's pretensions and of Mark's despair, Chuck was so simple, so human. She almost hugged him, but she just sat where she was. Later she called him and invited him up to New York, but she never revealed just how depressed she was. She couldn't drive. She couldn't go out. She couldn't initiate anything. All she did was work part-time as a reading teacher and come back and sit in her apartment on West End Avenue with her Wheaten Terrier, smoking pot and listening to Cat Stevens.

Her sister came from California. Even her mother got her doctor-boyfriend to try to intervene. Nothing worked. Beverly's pattern remained the same, except she started visiting Chuck every other weekend in DC.

If he wanted to take care of her, she would let him. He was a nurturing type. He taught her to drive. He cooked for her. He took her out with Marty and Claudia. He showed her the sights of Washington. He let her dog shit on his rug. They would sleep late Sunday mornings and then go out for brunch. He started looking for houses.

Her father had not been nurturing. He was an explosive Napoleon who got her mother out of Europe by some miracle. Her mother's parents—old, tired, bewildered—refused to go. They refused to believe the Czech government they had faithfully served would let anything happen to them. Her mother's brother stayed to take care of them. After they were sent to the camps to die, the brother was sent to Auschwitz to work, where he saw Herr Mengele, "The Angel of Death," every day.

Her uncle came to America after the war, a shell of the strong young man he had been. Beverly's father, a successful businessman before the war in Europe, had managed to put his money into diamonds and gold and literally dragged his spoiled wife all through France to get on the last ship out from Lisbon. He bribed and bullied his way past hundreds of ambivalent Frenchmen.

Her father personally renovated a factory in New Jersey that made toys. He then took over a bigger factory. He invested in IBM and, eventually, had a seat on the New York Stock Exchange. No, he was many things, but not nurturing.

Her mother was something else, a beautiful, graceful, mannered young lady, the product of years of civilized, cultivated Jewish life—the flower of Prague. Chuck called her "Marlene Dietrich." She was the consummate hostess. She had dinner parties for her fellow émigrés (including families who would produce Henry Kissinger and Henry Winkler), which were the talk of Forest Hills. She would tinkle her little dinner bell, and her faithful servant, Magdalena, would appear as if by magic—a gigantic horse of a woman who could have been, should have been, a nun. What she cooked and baked made the guests feel as if they were back in Austria, Hungary, or Czechoslovakia.

Mary had never rebelled openly like Beverly did. She had her books and her career hopes, and as soon as she could, she left. Beverly, more confrontational, never really got along with her mother and certainly did not always display good manners. When she was sixteen, her beloved father died of a stomach infection, leaving her at home with her mother for a nightmarish two years. Thank heaven for her stepfather, who was already courting his grief-stricken patient. Beverly was sent off to one of the Seven Sisters women's colleges, but she went with relief and joy.

So nurturing was not part of her background, not from her parents, not from her husband, and not from Mark.

She soaked up all she could from Chuck, and gradually she got better. And if he wanted to marry and have kids, fine, as ridiculously conventional as it seemed to her. Her healing continued. What was the price? Sex with Chuck was not disappointing. What he lacked in technique, he made up in enthusiasm.

Marty, who looked like a movie star and who liked to tease Chuck, once asked Chuck—who looked like a combination of Edward G. Robinson and Dustin Hoffman—what his secret was with women. Beverly was so glad Chuck had gotten him back by saying, "Marty, didn't you know that unlike some other guys, I'm good in bed?"

Oops! Beverly almost missed her turn. Her reverie over, she started looking for Claudia.

The Cafeteria and a Friend

Chuck sat down at a table with Marty. "Chuck, how's it going?"

Relaxed with his friend, Goldbug answered, "Not bad. Things are busy at work. Beverly told me she wants to go to a poetry workshop in Washington, Virginia for four weeks at the end of September."

"She's gone away before, hasn't she?" Marty inquired.

"Yes, we call it poetry camp. I'll tell you, Marty, she's so obsessed with this poetry thing. A couple nights every week, and then away during the summer and fall. At home, she stays in this one room with her computer and spends almost all of her time writing. Whenever the phone rings, she asks if it's Dick Cavett asking her to be on his show."

Marty laughingly said, "So, she is a bit grandiose?"

"Grandiose?" Chuck said. "That's an understatement. It's like all-consuming. The hierarchy at home is her writing, her friends, the kids, her thesaurus, her dog and then me ... and then the house."

"Well, at least you're not last!"

Chuck just blurted it out, "I don't feel I have a wife."

Marty tried to reassure him. "Well, in these times you're supposed to be supportive. Maybe if you took more of an interest."

"I have and I am. Sunday I went to her reading at the Salon."

In mock horror, Marty cried out, "What? You missed an Eagles game?"

Not admitting that the Eagles didn't play that Sunday, Chuck answered, "Marty, this makes the Eagles pale into insignificance."

"Especially during a losing season," Marty added. They both laughed.

Chuck continued, "I keep wondering if she has someone else."

"Well, she does ... her muse."

"No, Marty, I mean a real person."

Marty was serious. "Well, the key is, does she take her diaphragm?"

Chuck replied, "You know, I never even thought to look."

Slapping his head with his hand, Marty exclaimed, "You dummkopf, I know where Claudia's diaphragm is at all times. I know where her diaphragm is more than I know where she is."

A pensive Chuck answered, "Gosh, I can't even imagine things have gotten so bad that my wife is screwing somebody else."

Marty tried to be sympathetic. "Well, you know Beverly. She never lets the grass grow under her feet."

"No, she smokes it every night," Chuck exclaimed. They both laughed.

"Freedom"

On the way back to his office, Goldbug's beeper went off. He pulled over to a pay phone on the side of a road and dialed the number. "Dr. Goldbug here."

A female voice answered, "Dr. Goldbug, this is the nurse at the emergency room. Remember I was on duty two nights ago when you committed James Jefferson?"

"Oh, yes," he answered. "How are you?"

"I'm afraid I have some bad news for you."

"What?"

The nurse continued, "Earlier today they had a hearing on the unit. Mr. Apple made a passionate speech about civil liberties, and the examiner was so impressed by how James was doing on his Haldol that he released him."

"Oh, no!"

"It gets worse," she continued. "His mother came to pick him up. They had a fight in the taxi. Apparently, it escalated once they got home. The bottom line is he strangled her and stabbed himself and now they're both here in the ER dead."

"Oh, my God."

"Dr. Goldbug, you tried. You did what you could."

Sighing, he said, "Thanks for letting me know," and he hung up.

The Phone Call

On September 30, 1987, while playing Ping-Pong in the basement of his parents' house with his sons, Goldbug got the worst phone call of his life.

"Dr. Goldbug, this is Isaac Wasmuhler. I'm a police officer in Rappahannock County. I'm not sure how to tell you this. Something horrible has happened. Your wife was raped and murdered last night."

"Raped and murdered?" Goldbug felt dizzy. He focused on *raped* and *murdered* as going together, like cream cheese and bagel, love and marriage, salt and pepper, Tom and Jerry. He felt himself lapsing into irrationality.

He did not cry. Later, he would cry when they put her in the ground and the implacable forever, the irreversibility of it, hit him. It was all he could think about then. But now inside of him—welling up, surging—was a tremendous rage. What was Beverly doing in a rural, isolated house in the countryside, so vulnerable? What was she doing away from him in the first place? Chasing literary fame? Or was it all his fault that he had so messed up the marriage with his expectations that she was out having a good time? Who else was in that house, and who had done this terrible thing?

Poor Beverly. Poorer him. And what the hell was he gonna tell the kids?

The Decision

Marty and Chuck were back in the cafeteria arguing. "It's a crazy idea. You're not a cop. You're a forty-four-year-old psychiatrist."

"Will you cover?" Chuck asked.

"Yes, I will cover, but your patients are not the issue. So far you've handled this well. The funeral was dignified—letting the kids come was the right decision. You have a chance of getting through this, but taking off and leaving the kids and trying to be some sort of Columbo—"

"They have no clue up there. They're like Keystone Kops."

Exasperated, Marty asked, "So what are you doing to do?"

"I can't do anything worse. It's something I need to do."

Marty tried to talk his friend out of it. "It could be your reaction to her death that you feel you should have done something ... and now you're going up there out of guilt."

Chuck insisted, "I *do* feel guilty."

"And you're being impulsive running up there. If the people who did this are running around, you'd be in danger. The kids could really not bear losing their sole remaining parent."

"Marty, as usual, your arguments are very logical, and if this were intellectual stuff, you'd be right. But there's something else going on. I just can't let whoever did this get away with it."

"So it's revenge?" Marty asked. "You know, one of my old Lodge mentors has written on revenge as a defense against loss."

"You could be right, Marty, but my mourning will be done up there."

Rappahannock County

On Monday, July 24, 1749, a seventeen-year-old surveyor laid off a town in the Blue Ridge Mountains. It was a five-block by two-block grid. The streets bore the names Jett, Wheeler, Porter, and Calvert—the names of the families who lived on the land upon which the town was founded.

One of the main streets was named Gay Street. There was no Gay family. It was thought that the young surveyor named the street after the beautiful teenage girl Gay Fairfax, the cousin of his older brother's wife, who herself was the daughter of the powerful lord who managed this land.

In 1743 Augustine Washington had died. His son, Lawrence, a very promising young man, inherited his plantation at Hunting Creek and renamed it Mount Vernon after a former naval commander, a mentor of his, named Admiral Edward Vernon. He then married the daughter of the manager of the plantation next door, Ann Fairfax. Her father was William Fairfax, cousin and business agent of Thomas, the Sixth Lord Fairfax who had inherited 5.7 million acres of prime Virginia real estate south of the Potomac River from his mother's family, the Culpeppers.

After many years in England, eventually the unmarried Thomas came to live with his cousin William at William's plantation, Belvoir. In so doing, he came to know Lawrence's half brother George, who was a friend of William's son (Ann's brother), William George Fairfax. Lord Thomas Fairfax was said to have been pleased with George Washington's energy and talents. In 1748 he employed him and his cousin's son, William George, in a surveying expedition beyond the Blue Ridge Mountains. Then, in 1749, George William, having apparently supplanted his father as Lord Fairfax's agent, authorized his friend George Washington, then age seventeen, to lay out a town by the Rock River approximately twenty-six miles west of the town of Fairfax, which was later to have its name changed to Culpepper.

Thus it was on Monday, July 24, 1749, that George Washington, with two companions, laid off the town on a five by two block grid. One of the main streets was named after the beautiful Gay Fairfax, the only daughter of yet another cousin and business associate of Lord Fairfax by the name of Hampton Fairfax.

What went wrong between George and Gay, of whom George was extremely fond? It is known that George accompanied Lawrence to Barbados in 1751. Lawrence had come down with a severe case of tuberculosis and went south for his health. Not only didn't it work (both Lawrence and Ann were to die tragically within a couple of years), but George came down with smallpox soon after arriving in Barbados. He returned in 1752, his face very much disfigured. Family myth had it that Gay took one look at him, and that was the end of the courtship.

Historical speculation is that Lawrence was George's role model. If Lawrence had not come down with TB and then gone to Barbados, the first president of the United States might have been Lawrence Washington, and George might have married into the fabulously wealthy Fairfax clan as opposed to the less wealthy—but still well-fixed—Custis family, who had a widowed daughter named Martha.

The small town that George surveyed became the oldest of the twenty-eight towns in the United States named Washington. For the first forty-seven years of its existence, it was a trading post for the Monahoac Indians, who were not of the more common Powhatan tribe but were related in some way to the Sioux. It was recognized formally as a town by the Virginia House of Burgesses in 1796. It became a busy frontier crossroads for an intersecting stage route. It became a self-supporting community with blacksmiths, liveries, tanners, canneries, and ordinaries, or hotels. It was famous for berries in spring, peaches in summer, apples in the fall, and Xmas trees in the winter. The Rock River, one of the headwaters of the Rappahannock, an Indian name meaning "Rising Waters," formed the northern and eastern boundaries of the town. It was called Little Washington after Big Washington became the capital in 1800.

For more than 250 years, the town retained the same 5-block by 2-block configuration. The town fathers resisted development. In the Eisenhower era, it was briefly famous after an all-women slate of town council members defeated an allegedly do-nothing male city council in a last-minute political coup.

In 1975, *Meet The Press* commentator Bill Monroe hailed Little Washington's frugal management. He lived in the community of 190. The town council members got paid $5 a month but only if they attended the meetings. A sewer system was rejected as dangerously appealing to outsiders. In later years, it became famous for its five-star restaurant, The Inn at Little Washington.

Chuck knew that the retreat where Beverly was murdered was called Feathers, and it was located several miles outside of Little Washington. He had called the owner-manager, and she was expecting him, but first he wanted to check in with the police.

The Investigation

Sgt. Wasmuhler was a short, muscular young man with light hair, a fuzzy beard, and red cheeks. He did not look to be more than twenty, but he was at least thirty years old. "Doctor, the investigation is continuing. We did retrieve evidence at the crime scene."

"DNA?" Chuck asked.

"Yeah," the investigator answered.

"And Beverly was strangled. Right?"

"Yes, sir. That was what the medical examiner told us, and there were bruises and evidence of a struggle."

Chuck tried not to think about that. "Any progress at all?" he asked.

"No, sir," Wasmuhler continued. "We do have a roster of nearby individuals with prior convictions for sex crimes. We interviewed them, but they all have alibis."

"And you interviewed the people at the house?"

"Yes sir. The residents were all interviewed. They all claimed to be asleep when it happened. There were four of them"—Wasmuhler checked his notebook—"the female owner and three other guests, two male and one female."

"And you believe them?"

"Well, let me put it this way. There is no evidence to the contrary. The body was not found until the next morning. We did find that the window in her room was tampered with. There was evidence of footprints in the ground underneath the window."

Chuck persisted, "Did you take casts of the footprints?"

"No. We don't do that," Wasmuhler said.

"What about the DNA? Has it been sent to a lab?"

Wasmuhler patiently tried to answer all the questions. "No. It's registered and ready to be sent if we find the suspect."

Chuck needed further clarification. "But won't the DNA, if it hits a match, tell you who to suspect?"

"We don't have funds to test all the DNA."

"Any other similar crimes recently?"

"Yes," Wasmuhler said, "there was one rape by a masked man, very little to go on. And one hitchhiker was found strangled, but her body was so decomposed we couldn't tell if she was raped."

Chuck wanted to know how the police know the victim was a hitchhiker.

The investigator replied, "She was seen hitchhiking about six months before the body was found."

Chuck stood up. "So let me sum this up. My wife is dead ... killed in your town ... there are no active leads ... the DNA is untested ... and you don't do foot casts."

Wasmuhler tried to placate him. "Listen, we have a small department here. We do the best we—"

But Chuck was already out the door.

Feathers

It took only fifteen minutes to reach the small, white farmhouse with the wooden sign surrounded by feathers with the word *Feathers* engraved upon the wood. When Goldbug came to the door, he heard the bleating of goats in the backyard and headed off in that direction. He saw a small herd of brown goats, grey goats, and the occasional white goat swarming around a large woman dumping a powdery food into a trough. The owner, Franny Gross, looked like an aging hippie: long, scraggly grey hair, fleshy face, and a large, broad nose. She wore jeans and a beaded white shirt not quite covering a plus-size body.

She looked up and saw him. "Oh, you must be Beverly's husband. I'm so sorry."

"So am I," he said.

"I could never imagine such a thing happening here," she replied.

Just then, a loud, giggling group came bursting out the back door. Two men, one very tall and good-looking and the other a short, slender, effeminate man, were accompanied by a very attractive woman with dark hair dressed in a T-shirt and cutoffs with symmetrical thighs that stirred Goldbug's loins. He tried to avoid looking at her.

Franny introduced the gay guy as Freddie Cook, who seemed hypomanic, dancing around, gesturing with exaggerated mannerisms, not able to be still. The woman smiled at the tall man as she was introduced.

At once, Goldbug felt very uneasy. He had the instinctive awareness—not reduced by the tall man's steady gaze, clipped "Waspy" accent, and constantly bemused look—that something had gone on between this guy and Beverly. The woman didn't appear to be connected herself to the tall man, whose name was Malcolm Bishop. His writing program at the University of Iowa was very prestigious. She was reacting to something he had done.

Her name was Jessi—with an *i*—Black. Goldbug couldn't resist saying, "So you have three eyes?"

She quickly replied, "The better to see, my dear."

None of them was in mourning. But as if they all had the same thoughts—why he was there—they grew serious and expressed their condolences.

"Worst that ever happened."

"I couldn't believe it."

"What a waste."

Goldbug tried to empathize. "Must've been scary."

They were all poets. Jessi with an *i*, small and dark like Beverly, frenetic Freddie, and the tall, priapic Malcolm, who kept staring at Goldbug as if he were a lab animal.

It was very disconcerting. Goldbug regretted coming, especially when Franny left the goats to show him Beverly's room, where her body was found.

But it was more than that, more than Beverly's lingering presence. He was afraid what he would find out.

The first interview was with Franny. She took him through the white, wood-framed farmhouse. It had a huge kitchen, three bathrooms with old-fashioned fixtures, and five bedrooms—three on the second floor and two on the first floor. Beverly had had one of the downstairs bedrooms, along with Franny. Freddie, Malcolm, and Jessi slept upstairs.

Goldbug took a look at the window where the footprints were found, the window through which the intruder—the murderer—had climbed. Goldbug started to shake. He shut his mind off so as not to imagine what had actually happened there. here.

Franny described the program: a collegial, peer-centered, four-week session of poets critiquing each other's work. All of the poets had faculty appointments and had been published. Beverly herself had been an adjunct professor at American University. There were literary grants available at the State Cultural Foundation, and tuition for what was commonly called Poetry Camp was not hard to come by.

Franny was not a poet herself but a former English teacher who used the funds from her campers to supplement her income. The location in the Shenandoah Mountains between Washington and Sperryville, a pastoral setting with goats and green, open spaces, was conducive to a focus on one's muse.

Franny thought of herself as a head counselor who organized swimming and hiking trips and outings to antique places and historical houses such as Cedar Creek, the restored home of President Madison's sister who had married the scion of a Pennsylvania German pioneer family, one of the first to settle in the Virginia highlands.

Franny told Goldbug that the group his wife had been in, who was still there, had been one of her most enjoyable—not just due to the quality of the poetry, but due to the fun-loving personas of the people. She said Beverly and Jessi had been very close but that all of them seemed to really enjoy each other.

Goldbug asked to see Freddie next, judging that he would be the easiest source of information, which he was.

Goldbug first asked what was happening the night of the murder. Freddie told him that they had all gone to dinner at The Café, a trendy quiche and salad place in Washington. They came back and did what they usually did after dinner—go out on the porch and work on their poems. Franny had gone to dinner with them but was not on the porch. Most of the night was spent on each other's work. All of them talked, laughed, and critiqued until long after the sun went down. Freddie said he left first, but judging from the noise on the porch, Beverly, Jessi, and Malcolm worked for another hour.

Goldbug was silent, and Freddie blurted out, "I bet that's not all you want to know."

Goldbug remained silent.

Freddie continued, "I'll bet you want to know if your wife got involved with Malcolm. I'm really sorry to tell you this, but she did. Jessi kept egging her on. Jessi said she was the mother of the relationship and I was the father … and I had never been a father before."

Goldbug felt himself shrinking and getting sick. He felt so small, yet not as invisible and detached as he wanted to be.

Freddie went on. "Malcolm thought her work was constrained … too much following of the rules, not enough imagination. So he said he was trying to liberate her. Then she'd go to Jessi and tell her everything. She'd spend just as much time with Jessi as with Malcolm. If you ask me, Jessi was after her as much as Malcolm was. Jessi would make her tell her everything, and I'm not sure that Beverly wasn't involved with Jessi as well."

Goldbug finally escaped during a lull in Freddie's pressured speech caused by his finally taking a breath.

Freddie had arranged for Jessi to speak with Goldbug next. She was now wearing even less than before. Almost every movement and sentence was provocative, but Goldbug was incapable—actually impotent—of generating a rise. Jessi acknowledged working very closely with Beverly and said she really loved her way with words. And she said Beverly had talked about her husband a lot, though neglecting to say how much of it was positive.

Goldbug started sweating and could feel his heart beat faster. Was he going to meet with Malcolm, whom he wanted to kill? Or was he going to run away? Marty always told him he had more guts than brains.

Goldbug could feel his rage at Malcolm being projected into paranoia until he was convinced Malcolm was the root of all evil. Before he knew it, Malcolm was looming in front of him, dwarfing him, asking him into his room, the room where Beverly had done God knows what.

Goldbug started out, "So on the night Beverly was killed, when did you see her last?"

"We were on the porch discussing her work until about midnight. I didn't hear anything. The next day I woke up and was shocked."

"Was there anyone she met, anyone she had contact with even peripherally?"

"No, no one," Malcolm answered.

By keeping it mundane, Goldbug was trying to maintain his stability. He then decided to raise the stakes. "So, are you married?"

"Yes."

"Any kids?"

"Yes. One daughter and one granddaughter."

Goldbug wondered, "What does your wife do?"

"She teaches biology at the University of Iowa."

So, thought Goldbug, *vulnerability is not a one-way street.* "Getting back to Beverly, what kind of mood was she in that last night?"

Malcolm answered directly, "She was in a good mood. She was working hard. She took her work very seriously."

You're telling me! Goldbug thought. Finally, he had had enough of Malcolm's smugness and his arrogance, and he had to leave. "Well, I'll get back to you if there's anything else," he said.

Malcolm looked at him quizzically as he left.

The Pub

Goldbug fled the house, barely stopping to say good-bye to Franny. He drove his car almost mindlessly to the pub he remembered seeing in Little Washington. Sweating, feeling nauseous, he headed for the barstool and ordered two screwdrivers, which he drained in about ten minutes.

His heart was beating fast and loud. He kept asking himself, *How could Beverly had fallen for that pseudo classy asshole? Was it his looks? Was it his confidence? His Waspy sense of entitlement that this was his country and everybody else were just guests?*

He had just ordered two more screwdrivers when he heard a loud commotion. Two burly rednecks had parked their black pickup—strewn with confederate flags and pro-gun and anti-gay stickers—and barreled into the bar. They came up to the other end of the bar where Goldbug was standing. They were big, heavy guys with red faces, wide noses, short, blonde hair, and a light-haired stubble on their cheeks.

Holding their beer, which had magically appeared in their hands, suddenly they addressed Goldbug. "Ain't you," the closer one asked, "the guy whose wife was killed at the hippie house?"

Goldbug nodded, not looking at them. He wondered, *How did they know? Oh, shit! It's a small town. Maybe the cops or Franny?* He looked around the room. He was the only guy with long hair and a goatee.

The closer hulk then said, "That's what you get when you leave your husband and hang out with druggie hippies."

"Yeah, I'll bet they have orgies," the other one chimed in. "I bet they invited the rapist in."

44

At that moment, something in Goldbug snapped.

Despite his rational side saying, *They're trying to provoke you; just leave,* Goldbug threw the contents of his drink at the closer of the two behemoths and charged at him like a bull. He pinned the first guy against the bar with his shoulder. The second guy tore him away and threw him across the room.

It reminded him of a scene from the movie *The Frisco Kid,* where Gene Wilder slapped one of the three evil giant guys who had stolen all of his stuff; but now there was no Harrison Ford, the guy on the white horse, to save him. With every painful punch to his face, Goldbug felt the perverse gratification of punishment for his guilt at not protecting Beverly and not being such a compelling mate that she would not leave him, even for four weeks. But as his jaw started to hurt and he felt his nose bleed, he got mad.

He knew he should go down and stay down, but he couldn't. He got in a good left hook to the chin of Neanderthal number one, and then a good right to the soft belly of Neanderthal two. But the satisfaction was short-lived as he tumbled under a downpour of punches. Going down was no longer a matter of choice.

He heard a police siren and felt himself lifted into a police car. He remembered being asked if he would press charges, and he pridefully, spitefully, defiantly yelled out, "No!"

The Hospital

At the hospital, he was put on a gurney and became aware of a blonde-haired, busty, hippy nurse gently cleaning off the blood and applying some kind of antiseptic. She was not his normal type—the slim, petite, dark-haired girl who is smart and pert and sassy. She pushed him to x-ray and smiled a lot at him. When she moved his jaw, she said, "This is going to hurt you a lot more than it does me."

Goldbug laughed but then winced and said that it hurt to laugh. Xrays of his nose and jaw were negative, but he was glad they could not take xrays of his genitals because this nurse was definitely having an effect.

As she bandaged him up, she said, "I didn't know psychiatrists got into barroom brawls. What kind of therapy is that?"

He replied, "It was a psychiatric intervention against two guys who were too close to the dinosaurs."

"Is it always so painful to have a psychiatric intervention?" she asked.

Goldbug laughed. "Usually it's more painful for the patient than for the psychiatrist. Once a patient came in and sat down in my chair, and I knew immediately she was psychotic. I called the police to have them take her to the hospital. They said to me, 'How do you know she's psychotic?' I said, 'Because she's sitting in my chair.' So the cop said, 'Well, Doc, why don't you sit in another chair?'"

The nurse laughed, a wonderful sound, one of the nicest of the past month. She finished bandaging him up and then said, "Now don't let me see you here again or I'll report you to the Psychiatric Association."

"I'd like to see you again," Goldbug admitted.

The nurse remarked, "You know Washington is a small town. Everybody knows everyone else's business. Your wife's death was horrible. Then you came to find out what happened. A lot of people thought that was wrong or even ridiculous, but not me. I thought it was very loyal, unusual in these times, almost a throwback. It's the kind of loyalty I'd like to have someone display for me."

"How do you know it's loyalty?" Goldbug asked. "Maybe it's just guilt."

"In order to feel guilt, you have to really care."

"It's like a Woody Allen movie. I feel guilt before I feel love."

Laughingly, she said, "Woody Allen would never have attacked two big red-necks."

Goldbug continued, "Yeah, he restricts his aggression to Sunday school teachers and librarians."

The nurse was still laughing when she said, "You don't know my name."

Goldbug answered, "Yes, I do … Florence Nightingale."

"It's Jan. Jan Bloodworth."

"I'm Chuck Goldbug."

"I know," she said.

"When can you get off?" he inquired. Jan told him in an hour. "I'll wait." he said. Jan nodded.

That first night, they spent three hours talking. Goldbug told her about his marriage, about his sons, about his work, about his friends. She told him just a little more about her job. He finally walked her home and they agreed to see each other the next night.

Jan

On the second night, they met and walked all through the town.

"When I was fourteen, my dad left my mom," Jan said. "He basically ran away with his secretary, who was much younger. He remained a good dad. He would see us regularly and money was not a problem. But my mom basically collapsed and my sisters looked to me.

"I took care of them my whole teenage life. Between my family and school, I barely went out. I was the only girl in nursing school who thought it was liberating."

Chuck interjected. "Your parents really let you down."

Jan demurred. "They did their best. I mean, it goes back generations. My mom came from an alcoholic family. There was a lot of insecurity, and they were poor. My mom always looked better than she really was.

"The main problem was not school. I did fine there. The problem was I didn't get a chance to have much experience with guys. I kept them at arm's length. I was afraid of them and my reaction to them. I guess I was a bit naive. I was so innocent, so vulnerable.

"I met this medical student, Scott, at a party in nursing school. He was pretty, very smart, and aggressive. He made Alpha Omega Alpha—you know, the honorary society for the best and brightest medical students.

"In retrospect, and no surprise to you, he was a lot like my dad. Very focused on himself. Would you believe I went with him for six years, helping him, loving him, getting to know his family, where he was treated like a prince? All the way into his surgical residency. We even lived together.

"I was so stupid. I didn't even insist on an engagement ring. Just his words—always his words. I even paid one half of our apartment rent from my first job in Cincinnati, where I'm from.

"Then, after all that time, he met someone else. Can you believe it? He did to me what my dad did to my mom. She was a medical technician and younger than I. He left me a note after six years. Then he moved out and left me to pay the whole rent.

"I'm not giving you the whole picture. He could be very sweet. And he was so competent, like he could do anything."

Goldbug was upset. "Now I'm worried. I'm not blowing my horn. I was abusive to my wife. Like I told you—by fighting what she really wanted and not supporting her. But now I'm tired of these games. I just want to be really with someone. I'd probably be too nice. I wouldn't turn you on."

Jan moved closer and kissed him passionately on the lips. "I've had enough of that abuse stuff. I'm so tired of that. I don't want someone so great. It's not sustainable. I just want someone who wants to be with me, who thinks of me."

"Thanks a lot. Is it so obvious I'm not great?"

Jan laughed. "You said yourself you dress like Columbo. You said you walk like the Incredible Hulk. You glorify your flaws. That's why you're so accepting of your patients' flaws."

"Yeah, but you didn't have to believe all of it!" he retorted.

Jan kissed him again. "You love that I believe it. It takes all the pressure off. You're the anti-Scott. You don't care about your image. You try to do your best, but not all the time. You don't have to be perfect." She laughed. "Scott was perfect—for a while. He was imperfectly perfect. You're perfectly imperfect."

Laughing, he said, "How can you know me so well? You just met me."

Jan hugged him. "You're just what I want."

"But what if you get tired of my flaws?"

"I'll never get tired of your flaws. They're my security. They mean you can love me more than you love you."

"I like the way you think."

He spread his jacket on the ground. They were in a park and no one was around. They lay down together and tore at each other's clothes. They felt each other all over. He deliberately held himself back from entering her, not wanting to seem too selfish. She kissed him again, took hold of him, and pulled him into her. They both felt carried away to some magical place.

Afterward, they dressed and held onto each other. He said, "I haven't felt this good in God knows how long." She hugged him tighter.

Darren Mixley

The thin, dark-skinned young man slipped quietly out the door of the gatehouse, located between the stables and the stately antebellum mansion. He was dressed entirely in black, almost invisible in the moonless night. He fancied his dress to be like the Vietcong commandos who had ambushed his father.

His pace was rapid, and his mind was working just as fast. He reached into his pocket and took out two pictures, one of a smiling, white-haired, elderly black man, erect and muscular. and the other a younger version of the old man—unsmiling, intense, dressed in fatigues.

One hundred and fifty years ago, the Messenger farm had been the largest cotton plantation in Rappahannock county. The eighty-year-old matriarch who currently ran the place was the great-, great-, great-granddaughter of a cavalry officer who rode with Colonel Mosby. One-third of this land had been sold off for housing, but it was still a working farm that raised horses, hogs, soybeans, and corn.

Darren chuckled as he remembered how his granddaddy Simon— the blacksmith for the Messengers for more than fifty years—talked of how Miss Martha wanted him to drive her around like he was that damn house nigger in the movie *Driving Miss Daisy*. What Miss Martha did not know (and no one else either) was how much Simon Mixley hated white people. He sure did fool them with that smile and his mild disposition and his hard work. But he had taken secret pride in seeing his big, strong son, Mack, defy the local establishment in the 1960s by marching around with Stokely Carmichael and Rap Brown, never backing down and being arrested so many times that finally they told him either he would go to Vietnam or the state penitentiary.

But before he went to Vietnam, he did certain things. He married Darren's mother. He read up on the two famous Virginia slave revolts—the first led by Gabriel Prosser in Southampton County in 1800, and the second (and more famous, and also more deadly) led by Nat Turner in Henrico County in 1831. The last thing he did was talk to his dad about taking care of the baby Darren if anything happened to him.

Mack Mixley was killed in Vietnam in 1967. The baby was ten months old. His widow threw the medals on the ground and started to drink. She ran to Richmond to become a party girl. That's why there was no picture of Dionne Mixley in Darren's pocket. He regarded his mother as the alcoholic tramp who threw him away.

When he was five, he heard that his mother had been murdered in a crack house when she refused to run the train. He felt nothing. For Darren, both mother and father were incorporated in his beloved granddad Simon, who taught him everything he knew.

When his granddaddy told him about white slave owners using black girls as sexual slaves, he got mad. He vowed that he himself would do the same to white girls some day. But Simon had only recently died in January 1987. He could not do what he thought of doing while his granddaddy was alive. His granddad would not have liked to see him risk getting into trouble. But since his granddaddy's death, he had done it three times, and tonight was going to be the fourth. The first was a hitchhiker. He grew bolder and wore a mask to do the second girl at her home. The third was less than a month ago at the hippie house. He had not worn a mask then. He had an eye on a fourth girl. He had seen her while driving Miss Martha around town, the pretty, red-haired white girl walking into her house. He knew exactly where she lived.

His granddaddy had personally taught him how to drive, and Miss Martha had liked the idea of him driving her. He had been her chauffeur for three years. He was proud of his driving. He had never gotten a ticket. He wondered if they gave tickets for rape and murder.

He still had another mile and a half to walk until he reached the town.

The Plan

On the third night, Chuck told Jan about his plan. He knew she might think it was crazy, but he still wanted to do it and he wanted her to do it with him. She said it was a crazy idea but she would do it so he wouldn't have to do it alone. So they both patrolled the town late at night, hoping to capture the rapist in the act, identify him, and take him to the county police. He felt a surge of warm feeling he hadn't had for a while.

The first three nights they did it nothing happened, but they enjoyed being with each other. They saw lovers, drunks, and teenagers, and they talked and they talked. But the fourth night, the sixth night of their time together, was different.

At around 2 AM, they were crossing an alley behind the natural food store, The Southern Kernel, they heard the sound of a window opening, so they went toward the sound. They were in the shadows and could not be seen. On the bottom floor of a three-story apartment building, they saw a thin black man, dressed in all black, about to climb through a window.

Goldbug, brandishing a thick club of wood, ran toward the window and tackled the guy. A red-haired young woman leaned out the window and screamed. The intruder, though thin and wiry, was strong, and he pushed Goldbug off. Goldbug then hit him below the knee. The guy staggered, and then cursed and started to limp away. Goldbug hit him in the same spot again, and he crumpled to the ground. Goldbug dropped the wood and got the guy in a headlock, but he was slippery and he punched Goldbug hard in his crotch.

Goldbug groaned and released him. The young man got on top of him and was choking him when Jan came up behind him with the wooden club Goldbug had dropped and hit the man on the top of his head with all her might. He immediately fell limp, letting go of Goldbug's neck and rolling onto the ground. He was silent and motionless, with blood dripping from his scalp. Goldbug, trying to catch his breath, got to his knees.

In the distance, he heard a siren. Apparently, the girl who was about to be attacked had called the police. Goldbug said to the police when they arrived, "There's the guy that killed my wife."

A New Life

Three months passed. Bart and Jason are throwing a football in a park. A slimmer Chuck walks arm in arm with Jan. The sun is shining. An aura of contentment surrounds all four of them. Even the dog, who keeps jumping up trying to intercept the boys' passes, is happy. The boys tease their father that Mona, the dog, is better than the Eagles' cornerbacks, especially one nicknamed "Toast" for all the times he was burned.

Chuck was all cried out. He was emotionally spent. All the sadness, guilt, anger … it still came back periodically, but not with the same intensity. Jan helped a lot. And that was something he did not feel guilty about.

Despite Marty's relentless and annoying comments—"Well, you're not supposed to enjoy Jan; if you do, it would mean you wanted Beverly dead or even that you killed her"—Chuck was happy. He knew that Marty said those things to help him, but he felt that Marty overestimated him. He would never feel guilty about Jan, no matter whose death enabled their relationship.

He thought of David Kennedy, who was thirteen when he was sent to European summer camp two months after his father was killed in Los Angeles. When the sexy French teenagers found out who he was, they couldn't keep their hands off him. He had an incredible summer and he felt so much guilt because it meant part of him wanted his beloved father to die so he could have sex with any sultry French girl he wanted. That guilt led to his opiate addiction and to his death ten years later.

Chuck thought that David Kennedy, drug addict, lover of Rachel Ward, houseguest of a Harvard psychiatrist whose treatment of him as a special patient led to his demise, had more of a conscience than he did.

But Chuck never had trouble acknowledging his flaws. Some said he was too accepting of them. But the tragedy of Beverly's death had one lingering effect: he did not want to go anywhere. He just wanted to stay close to his house, close to Jan, and close to the boys.

My God, he said to himself, *I've become like Mrs. Harrison.*

About the Author

After Temple University medical school, a psychiatric residency, and service in the U.S. Army, Chuck Goldberg started a private practice in adult and adolescent psychiatry, and became board-certified in both.

He published a journal article on Adolescent School Phobia, and he presented a paper to a national meeting of adolescent psychiatrists on "Freud Meets Bill: The Similarities between the Twelve Steps of AA and Dynamic Psychiatry."

The characters in this novella were crafted with insights from forty years of the author's psychiatric practice. The story is loosely based on real events. Names have been changed to protect the guilty.